THIS SUPER-BOOK
BELONGS TO

....

For Hugo, Lulah and Marla
- MC

For my daughter Eva, please NEVER be too old for a cuddle
- EP

First published in the United Kingdom in 2021 by Lantana Publishing Ltd.
www.lantanapublishing.com | info@lantanapublishing.com

American edition published in 2021 by Lantana Publishing Ltd., UK.

Text © Michael Catchpool, 2021
Illustration © Emma Proctor, 2021

Distributed in the United States and Canada by Lerner Publishing Group, Inc.
241 First Avenue North, Minneapolis, MN 55401 U.S.A.
For reading levels and more information, look for this title at www.lernerbooks.com
Cataloging-in-Publication Data Available.

Hardback ISBN: 978-1-911373-55-1
eBook PDF: 978-1-911373-95-7
ePub3: 978-1-913747-54-1

Printed and bound in China
Original artwork created in pencil, colored digitally.

SUPERJOE DOES NOT DO CUDDLES

Michael Catchpool

Emma Proctor

 Lantana

SuperJoe was up and ready to go. He had a busy day ahead of him.
It's not easy being a superhero, you know.

His mom was ready as well: ready to give him a great big cuddle before he went out.

"Superheroes **don't** do cuddles!" said SuperJoe. "What were you thinking? I've got people to save. There's a terrifying tiger on the loose!"

"Well, you're not going out without your scarf," said Mom.
"You'll catch a nasty chill."

SuperJoe was not impressed.

"What use is a scarf to a superhero, especially when you're catching ferocious tigers?"

But Mom wouldn't take no for an answer... so he had to wear it.

Off went SuperJoe to save some anxious tourists who had just had an unexpected encounter with a very hungry tiger.

"My superhero senses tell me that my arch-enemy the Gray Shadow has been making mischief," said SuperJoe. "That tiger didn't get here on its own!"

SuperJoe didn't mess about — superheroes don't. He dealt with the tiger
just like that and led it back to the wild where it belonged...

...and was home in time for dinner.

SuperJoe had no time to waste. He was
needed urgently. "I'm off!" he said.

"Not before you've had a cuddle with your mom!"

"Superheroes **don't** do cuddles!" said SuperJoe.
"I've got a runaway train to deal with! The engine's
going one way and the carriages the other."

"Well, you're not going out without your vest.
I don't want you getting cold!"

"What use is a vest to a superhero?" said SuperJoe.
"Especially when you've got terrible troubles with transport?"

But Mom wouldn't take no for an answer...
so he had to wear it.

SuperJoe shot off — as only a superhero can. "Call it super-intuition, but I think my evil nemesis the Gray Shadow has something to do with this," said SuperJoe.

And then he set about sorting out the runaway train and getting things back on track.

SuperJoe was so efficient, he even got the train to the station five minutes before it was actually due...

...and was home in time
for a long, hot soak
in the bath.

SuperJoe was raring to go – there was an emergency.
Emergencies are what superheroes do best.

"Don't forget a cuddle before you go," said Mom.

"If I've told you once, I've told you a thousand times:
superheroes **don't** do cuddles. Not even one!"

"Well you're not going out like that – just look at those underpants!"

"They're not my underpants, they're my superhero shorts!"

"They look like underpants to me," said Mom. "You need a belt to keep them up."

"What use is a belt when you've got to save people from a collapsing bridge, over a raging river, deep in the jungle?"

But Mom wouldn't take no for an answer...so he had to wear it.

"I spot the wicked hand of my foe the Gray Shadow at work here! Bridges over raging rivers in deep, dark jungles don't go collapsing on their own, you know."

SuperJoe set about a super-rescue... and he didn't even stop to sign autographs.

And though there were a lot of people to save...

...he made it back in time for bed.

"There have been far too many perilous predicaments and dangerous goings on recently. I really want to give someone a piece of my mind!" said SuperJoe.

"Not tonight, you won't," said Mom. "It's bedtime."

And she turned off the light.

But SuperJoe couldn't sleep.
He lay all alone in the dark, turning this way and that.

Until Mom came in.

"You need a warm, milky drink — that always helps."

"Superheroes don't do warm, milky drinks," said SuperJoe.

"Well, what about a song?"

"No silly lullabies or counting sheep or anything like that!"

"Then what do you need?" asked Mom.

"Just one thing." And SuperJoe whispered in Mom's ear.

"But... I thought superheroes definitely didn't do..."

"Ssshh," said SuperJoe quietly, "don't tell everyone!

I mean, what would the Gray Shadow say?"